McBROOM'S
WONDERFUL
ONE-ACRE
FARM

ILLUSTRATED BY
QUENTIN BLAKE

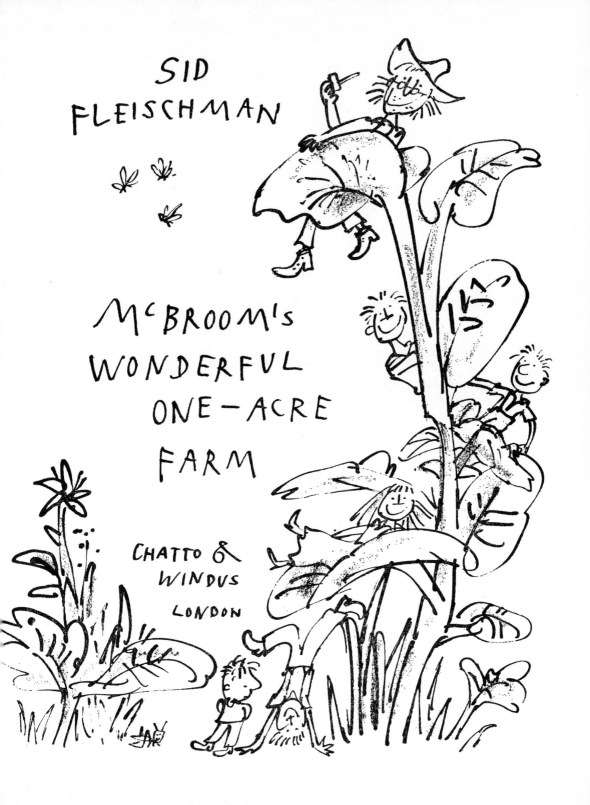

SID
FLEISCHMAN

McBROOM'S
WONDERFUL
ONE-ACRE
FARM

CHATTO &
WINDUS
LONDON

First published in the U.S.A. by
W. W. Norton & Company Inc., New York

First published in Great Britain 1972 by
Chatto & Windus Ltd., 42 William IV Street,
London WC2N 4DF

ISBN 0 7011 0486 4

Text copyrights © 1966, 1967, 1969, 1972
by Sid Fleischman

Illustrations copyright © 1972 by Quentin Blake

Printed in Great Britain by
Cox & Wyman Ltd, London, Fakenham and Reading.

CONTENTS

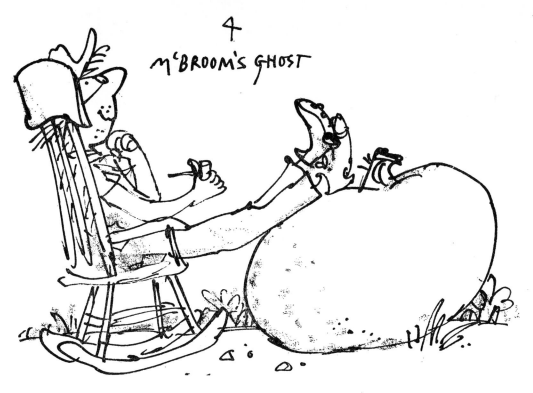

McBROOM TELLS THE TRUTH

There has been so much tomfool nonsense told about Mc-Broom's wonderful one-acre farm that I had better set matters straight. I'm McBroom. Josh McBroom. I'll explain about the water-melons in a minute.

I aim to put down the facts, one after the other, the way things happened – exactly.

It began, you might say, the day we left the farm in Connecticut. We piled our youngsters and everything we owned in our old air-cooled Franklin automobile. We headed West.

To count noses, in addition to my own, there was my dear wife Melissa and our eleven red-headed youngsters. Their names were Will*jill*hester*chester*peter*polly*timtommary*larry*and little*clarinda*.

It was summer, and the trees along the way were full of birdsong. We had got as far as Iowa when my dear wife Melissa made a startling discovery. We had *twelve* children along – one too many! She had just counted them again.

I slammed on the brakes and raised a cloud of dust.

"Willjillhesterchesterpeterpollytimtommarylarryandlittleclarinda!" I shouted. "Line up!"

The youngsters tumbled out of the car. I counted noses and there were twelve. I counted again. Twelve. It was a baffler as all the faces were familiar. Once more I made the count – but this time I caught Larry slipping around behind. He was having his nose counted twice, and the mystery was solved. The scamp! Didn't we laugh, though, and stretch our legs into the bargain.

Just then a thin, long-legged man came ambling down the road. He was so scrawny I do believe he could have hidden behind a flagpole, ears and all. He wore a tall stiff collar, a diamond pin in his tie, and a straw hat.

"Lost, neighbour?" he asked, spitting out the pips of a green apple he was eating.

"Not a bit," I said. "We're heading West, sir. We gave up our farm – it was half rocks and the other half tree-stumps.

8

Folks tell us there's land out West and the sun shines in the winter."

The stranger pursed his lips. "You can't beat Iowa for farmland," he said.

"Maybe so," I nodded. "But I'm short of funds. Unless they're giving farms away in Iowa we'll keep a-going."

The man scratched his chin. "See here, I've got more land than I can plough. You look like nice folks. I'd like to have you for neighbours. I'll let you have eighty acres cheap. Not a stone or a tree-stump anywhere on the place. Make an offer."

"Thank you kindly, sir," I smiled. "But I'm afraid you would laugh at me if I offered you everything in my leather purse."

"How much is that?"

"Ten dollars exactly."

"Sold!" he said.

Well, I almost choked with surprise. I thought he must be joking, but quick as a flea he was scratching out a deed on the back of an old envelope.

"Hector Jones is my name, neighbour," he said. "You can call me Heck – everyone does."

Was there ever a more kindly and generous man? He signed the deed with a flourish, and I gladly opened the clasp of my purse.

Three milky white moths flew out. They had been gnawing on the ten dollar bill all the way from Connecticut, but enough remained to buy the farm. And not a stone or tree-stump on it!

Mr. Heck Jones jumped on the running-board and guided

us a mile up the road. My youngsters tried to amuse him along the way. Will wiggled his ears, and Jill crossed her eyes, and Chester twitched his nose like a rabbit, but I reckoned Mr. Jones wasn't used to youngsters. Hester flapped her arms like a bird, Peter whistled through his front teeth, which were missing, and Tom tried to stand on his head in the back of the car. Mr. Heck Jones ignored them all.

Finally he raised his long arm and pointed.

"There's your property, neighbour," he said.

Didn't we tumble out of the car in a hurry? We gazed with delight at our new farm. It was broad and sunny, with an oak tree on a gentle hill. There was one defect, to be sure. A boggy-looking pond spread across an acre beside the road. You could lose a cow in a place like that, but we had got a bargain – no doubt about it.

"Mama," I said to my dear Melissa. "See that fine old oak on the hill? That's where we'll build our farmhouse."

"No you won't," said Mr. Heck Jones. "That oak ain't on your property. All that's yours is what you see under water. Not a rock or a tree-stump in it, like I said."

I thought he must be having his little joke, except that there wasn't a smile to be found on his face. "But, *sir!*" I said. "You clearly stated that the farm was eighty acres."

"That's right."

"That marshy pond hardly covers an acre."

"That's wrong," he said. "There are a full eighty acres – one piled on the other, like griddle cakes. I didn't say your farm was all on the surface. It's eighty acres deep, McBroom. Read the deed."

I read the deed. It was true.

11

"*Hee-haw! Hee-haw!*" he snorted. "I got the best of you, McBroom! Good day, neighbour."

He scurried away, laughing up his sleeve all the way home. I soon learned that Mr. Heck was always laughing up his sleeve. Folks told me that when he'd hang up his coat and go to bed, all that stored-up laughter would pour out of his sleeve and keep him awake nights. But there's no truth to that.

I'll tell you about the water-melons in a minute.

Well, there we stood gazing at our one-acre farm that wasn't good for anything but jumping into on a hot day. And that day was the hottest I could remember. The hottest on record, as it turned out. That was the day, three minutes before noon, when the cornfields all over Iowa exploded into popcorn. That's history. You must have read about that. There are pictures to prove it.

I turned to our children. "Will*jill*hester*chester*peter*polly*-tim*tom*mary*larry*andlittle*clarinda*," I said. "There's always a bright side to things. That pond we bought is a mite muddy but it's wet. Let's jump in and cool off."

That idea met with favour and we were soon in our swimming togs. I gave the signal, and we took a running jump. At that moment such a dry spell struck that we landed in an acre of dry earth. The pond had evaporated. It was very surprising.

My boys had jumped in head first and there was nothing to be seen of them but their legs kicking in the air. I had to pluck them out of the earth like carrots. Some of my girls

were still holding their noses. Of course, they were sorely disappointed to have that swimming hole pulled out from under them.

But the moment I ran the topsoil through my fingers, my farmer's heart skipped a beat. That pond bottom felt as soft and rich as black silk. "My dear Melissa!" I called. "Come look! This topsoil is so rich it ought to be kept in a bank."

I was in a sudden fever of excitement. That glorious top-soil seemed to cry out for seed. My dear Melissa had a sack of dried beans along, and I sent Will and Chester to fetch it. I saw no need to bother ploughing the field. I directed Polly to draw a straight furrow with a stick and Tim to follow her, poking holes in the ground. Then I came along. I dropped a bean in each hole and stamped on it with my heel.

Well, I had hardly gone a couple of yards when something green and leafy tangled my foot. I looked behind me. There was a beanstalk travelling along in a hurry and looking for a pole to climb on.

"Glory be!" I exclaimed. That soil was *rich!* The stalks were spreading out all over. I had to rush along to keep ahead of them.

By the time I got to the end of the furrow the first stalks had blossomed, and the pods had formed, and they were ready for picking.

You can imagine our excitement. Will's ears wiggled. Jill's eyes crossed. Chester's nose twitched. Hester's arms

flapped. Peter's missing front teeth whistled. And Tom stood on his head.

"Willjillhesterchesterpeterpollytimtommarylarryandlittle-clarinda," I shouted. "Harvest them beans!"

Within an hour we had planted and harvested that entire crop of beans. But was it hot working in the sun! I sent Larry to find a good acorn along the road. We planted it, but it didn't grow near as fast as I had expected. We had to wait an entire three hours for a shade tree.

We made camp under our oak tree, and the next day we drove to Barnsville with our crop of beans. I traded it for various seeds – carrot and beet and cabbage and other items. The storekeeper found a few kernels of corn that hadn't popped, at the very bottom of the bin.

But we found out that corn was positively dangerous to plant. The stalk shot up so fast it would skin your nose.

Of course, there was a secret to that topsoil. A government man came out and made a study of the matter. He said there had once been a huge lake in that part of Iowa. It had taken thousands of years to shrink up to our pond, as you can imagine. The lake fish must have got packed in worse than sardines. There's nothing like fish to put nitrogen in the soil. That's a scientific fact. Nitrogen makes things grow to beat all. And we did occasionally turn up a fish-bone.

It wasn't long before Mr. Heck Jones came round to pay us a neighbourly call. He was eating a raw turnip. When he saw the way we were planting and harvesting cabbage his eyes popped out of his head. It almost cost him his eyesight.

He scurried away, muttering to himself.

"My dear Melissa," I said. "That man is up to mischief."

Folks in town had told me that Mr. Heck Jones had the worst farmland in Iowa. He couldn't give it away. Tornado winds had carried off his topsoil and left the hardpan right on top. He had to plough it with wedges and a sledge-hammer. One day we heard a lot of booming on the other side of the hill, and my youngsters went up to see what was happening. It turned out he was planting seeds with a shotgun.

Meanwhile, we went about our business on the farm. I don't mind saying that before long we were showing a handsome profit. Back in Connecticut we had been lucky to harvest one crop a year. Now we were planting and harvesting three, four crops a *day*.

But there were things we had to be careful about. Weeds, for one thing. My youngsters took turns standing weed guard. The instant a weed popped out of the ground, they'd race to it and hoe it to death. You can imagine what would happen if weeds ever got going in rich soil like ours.

We also had to be careful about planting-time. Once we planted lettuce just before my dear Melissa rang the bell for dinner. While we ate, the lettuce headed up and went to seed. We lost the whole crop.

One day back came Mr. Heck Jones with a grin on his face. He had figured out a loop-hole in the deed that made the farm ours.

"*Hee-haw!*" he laughed. He was munching a radish. "I got the best of you now, Neighbour McBroom. The deed says you were to pay me *everything* in your purse, and you *didn't*."

"On the contrary, sir," I answered. "Ten dollars. There wasn't another cent in my purse."

"There were *moths* in the purse. I seen 'em flutter out. Three milky white moths, McBroom. I want three moths by three o'clock this afternoon, or I aim to take back the farm. *Hee-haw!*"

And off he went, laughing up his sleeve.

Mama was just ringing the bell for dinner so we didn't have much time. Confound that man! But he did have his legal point. "Willjillhesterchesterpeterpollytimtommarylarryand littleclarinda!" I said. "We've got to catch three milky white moths! Hurry!"

We hurried in all directions. But moths are next to impossible to locate in the day-time. Try it yourself. Each of us came back empty-handed.

My dear Melissa began to cry, for we were sure to lose our farm. I don't mind telling you that things looked dark. Dark! That was it! I sent the youngsters running down the road to a lonely old pine tree and told them to rush back with a bushel of pine cones.

Didn't we get busy though! We planted a pine cone every three feet. They began to grow. We stood around anxiously, and I kept looking at my pocket watch. I'll tell you about the water-melons in a moment.

Sure enough, by ten minutes to three, those cones had grown into a thick pine forest.

It was dark inside, too! Not a ray of sunlight slipped through the green pine boughs. Deep in the forest I lit a lantern. Hardly a minute passed before I was surrounded by milky white moths – they thought it was night. I caught three on the wing and rushed out of the forest.

There stood Mr. Heck Jones with the sheriff.

"*Hee-haw! Hee-haw!*" old Heck laughed. He was eating a quince apple. "It's nigh on to three o'clock, and you can't catch moths in the day-time. The farm is mine!"

"Not so fast, Neighbour Jones," said I, with my hands cupped together. "Here are the three moths. Now, skedaddle, sir, before your feet take root and poison ivy grows out of your ears!"

He scurried away, muttering to himself.

"My dear Melissa," I said. "That man is up to mischief. He'll be back."

It took a good bit of work to clear the timber, I'll tell you.
We had some of the pine milled and built ourselves a house
on the corner of the farm. What was left we gave away to our
neighbours. We were weeks blasting the roots out of the ground.

But I don't want you to think there was nothing but work
on our farm. Some crops we grew just for the fun of it. Take

19

pumpkins. The vines grew so fast we could hardly catch the pumpkins. It was something to see. The youngsters used to wear themselves out running after those pumpkins. Sometimes they'd have pumpkin races.

Sunday afternoons, just for the sport of it, the older boys would plant a pumpkin seed and try to catch a ride. It wasn't easy. You had to grab hold the instant the blossom dropped off and the pumpkin began to swell. Whoosh! It would yank you off your feet and take you whizzing over the farm until it wore itself out. Sometimes they'd use banana squash which was faster.

And the girls learned to ride corn stalks like pogo-sticks. It was just a matter of standing over the kernel as the stalk came busting up through the ground. It was good for quite a bounce.

We'd see Mr. Heck Jones standing on the hill in the distance, watching. He wasn't going to rest until he had prised us off our land.

Then, late one night, I was awakened by a hee-hawing outside the house. I went to the window and saw old Heck in the moonlight. He was cackling and chuckling and heeing and hawing and sprinkling seed every which way.

I pulled off my sleeping-cap and rushed outside.

"What mischief are you up to, Neighbour Jones!" I shouted.

"*Hee-haw!*" he answered, and scurried away, laughing up his sleeve.

I had a sleepless night, as you can imagine. The next morning, as soon as the sun came up, that farm of ours broke out in weeds. You never saw such weeds! They heaved out of the ground and tumbled madly over each other – chickweed, and milkweed, thistles and wild morning glory. In no time at all the weeds were in a tangle several feet thick and still rising.

We had a fight on our hands, I tell you! "Willjill-hesterchesterpeterpollytimtommarylarryandlittleclarinda!" I shouted. "There's work to do!"

21

We started hoeing and hacking away. For every weed we uprooted, another re-seeded itself. We were a solid month battling those weeds. If our neighbours hadn't pitched in to help, we'd still be there burning weeds.

The day finally came when the farm was cleared and up popped old Heck Jones. He was eating a big slice of watermelon. That's what I was going to tell you about.

"Howdy, Neighbour McBroom," he said. "I came to say goodbye."

"Are you leaving, sir?" I asked.

"No, but *you* are."

I looked him squarely in the eye. "And if I don't, sir?"

"Why, *hee-haw*, McBroom! There's heaps more of weed seed where that came from!"

My dander was up. I rolled back my sleeves, meaning to give him a whipping he wouldn't forget. But what happened next saved me the bother.

As my youngsters gathered around, Mr. Heck Jones made the mistake of spitting out a mouthful of water-melon seeds.

Things did happen fast!

Before I had quite realized what he had done, a water-melon vine whipped up around old Heck's scrawny legs and jerked him off his feet. He went whizzing every which way over the farm. Water-melon seeds were flying. Soon he came zipping back and collided with a pumpkin left over from Sunday. In no time water-melons and pumpkins went galloping all over the place, and they were knocking him about something wild. He streaked here and there. Melons crashed and exploded. Old Heck was so covered with melon pulp he looked like he had been shot out of a sauce bottle.

It was something to see. Will stood there wiggling his ears. Jill crossed her eyes. Chester twitched his nose. Hester flapped her arms like a bird. Peter whistled through his front teeth, which had grown in. Tom stood on his head. And little Clarinda took her first step.

By then the water-melons and pumpkins began to play themselves out. I figured Mr. Heck Jones would like to get home as fast as possible. So I asked Larry to fetch me the seed of a large banana.

"*Hee-haw!* Neighbour Jones," I said, and pitched the seed at his feet. I hardly had time to say goodbye before the vine had him. A long banana squash gave him a fast ride all the way home. I wish you could have been there to see it. He never came back.

That's the entire truth of the matter. Anything else you hear about McBroom's wonderful one-acre farm is an outright fib.

24

McBROOM AND THE BIG WIND

I can't deny it – it does get a mite windy out here on the prairie. Why, just last year a blow came ripping across our farm and carried off a pail of sweet milk. The next day it came back for the cow.

But that wasn't the howlin', scowlin', all mighty *big* wind I aim to tell you about. That was just a common little prairie

25

breeze. No account, really. Hardly worth bragging about.

It was the *big* wind that broke my leg. I don't expect you to believe that – yet. I'd best start with some smaller weather and work up to that bone-breaker.

I remember distinctly the first prairie wind that came scampering along after we bought our wonderful one-acre farm. My, that land is rich. Best topsoil in the country. There isn't a thing that won't grow in our rich topsoil, and fast as lightning.

The morning I'm talking about, our oldest boys were helping me to shingle the roof. I had bought a keg of nails, but it turned out those nails were a whit short. We buried them in our wonderful topsoil and watered them down. In five or ten minutes those nails grew a full half-inch.

So there we were, up on the roof, hammering down shingles. There wasn't a cloud in the sky at first. The younger boys were shooting marbles all over the farm and the girls were jumping rope. When I had pounded down the last shingle I said to myself, "Josh McBroom, that's a mighty stout roof. It'll last a hundred years."

Just then I felt a small draught on the back of my neck. A moment later one of the girls – it was Polly, as I recall – shouted up to me. "Pa," she said, "do jack rabbits have wings?"

I laughed. "No, Polly."

"Then how come there's a flock of jack rabbits flying over the house?"

I looked up. Mercy! Rabbits were flapping their ears across the sky in a perfect V formation, northbound. I knew then we were in for a slight blow.

26

"Run, everybody!" I shouted to the young 'uns. I didn't want the wind picking them up by the ears. "Will*jill*hester-*chester*peter*polly*tim*tom*mary*larry*andlittle*clarinda* – in the house! Scamper!"

The clothes-line was already beginning to whip around like a jump rope. My dear wife, Melissa, who had been baking a heap of biscuits, threw open the door. In we dashed and not a moment too soon. The wind was snapping at our heels like a pack of wolves. It aimed to barge right in and make itself at home! A prairie wind has no manners at all.

We slammed the door in its teeth. Now, the wind didn't take that politely. It rammed and battered at the door while all of us pushed and shoved to hold the door shut. My, it was a battle! How the house creaked and trembled!

"Push, my lambs," I yelled. "Shove!"

At times the door planks bent like barrel staves. But we held that roaring wind out. When it saw there was no getting past us, the zephyr sneaked around the house to the back door. Howsoever, our oldest boy, Will, was too smart for it. He piled Mama's heap of fresh biscuits against the back door. My dear wife, Melissa, is a wonderful cook, but her biscuits *are* terrible heavy. They made a splendid door-stop.

But what worried me most was our wondrous rich top-soil. That thieving wind was apt to make off with it, leaving us with a trifling hole in the ground.

"Shove, my lambs!" I said. "Push!"

The battle raged on for an hour. Finally the wind gave up butting its fool head against the door. With a great angry sigh it turned and whisked itself away, scattering fence posts as it went.

27

We all took a deep breath and I opened the door a crack. Hardly a leaf now stirred on the ground. A bird began to twitter. I rushed outside to our poor one-acre farm.

Mercy! What I saw left me pop-eyed. "Melissa!" I shouted with glee. "Willjillhesterchesterpeterpollytimtommarylarry-andlittleclarinda! Come here, my lambs! Look!"

We all gazed in wonder. Our topsoil was still there – every bit. Bless those youngsters! The boys had left their marbles all over the field, and the marbles had grown as large as boulders. There they sat, huge agates and sparkling glassies, holding down our precious topsoil.

But that rambunctious wind didn't leave empty-handed. It ripped off our new shingle roof. Pulled out the nails, too. We found out later the wind had shingled every burrow in the next county.

Now that was a strong draught. But it wasn't a *big* wind. Nothing like the kind that broke my leg. Still, that prairie gust was an education to me.

"Young 'uns," I said, after we'd rolled those giant marbles down the hill. "The next uninvited breeze that comes along, we'll be ready for it. There are two sides to every flapjack. It appears to me the wind can be downright useful on our farm if we let it know who's boss."

The next gusty day that came along, we put it to work for us. I made a wind plough. I rigged a bed-sheet and tackle to our old farm plough. Soon as a breeze sprung up I'd go tacking to and fro over the farm, ploughing as I went. Our son Chester once ploughed the entire farm in under three minutes.

On Thanksgiving morning Mama told the girls to pluck

a large turkey for dinner. They didn't much like that chore, but a prairie gust arrived just in time. The girls stuck the turkey out of the window. The wind plucked that turkey clean, feathers and all.

Oh, we got downright glad to see a blow come along. The young 'uns were always wanting to go out and play in the wind, but Mama was afraid they'd be carried off. So I made them wind-shoes – made 'em out of heavy iron skillets. Out in the breeze those shoes felt light as feathers. The girls would jump rope with the clothes-line. The wind spun the rope, of course.

Many a time I saw the youngsters put on their wind-shoes and go clumping outside with a big tin funnel and all the empty bottles and jugs they could round up. They'd cork the containers jam-full of prairie wind.

Then, come summer, when there wasn't a breath of air, they'd uncork a bottle or two of fresh winter wind and enjoy the cool breeze.

Of course, we had to wind-proof the farm every fall. We'd plant the field in buttercups. My, they were slippery – all that butter, I guess. The wind would slip and slide over the farm without being able to get a purchase of the topsoil. By then the boys and I had re-shingled the roof. We used screws instead of nails.

Mercy! Then came the *big* wind!

It started out gently enough. There were a few jack rabbits and some crows flying backwards through the air. Nothing out of the ordinary.

Of course the girls went outside to jump the clothes-line and the boys got busy laying up bottles of wind for summer. Mama had just baked a batch of fresh biscuits. My, they did smell good! I ate a dozen or so hot out of the oven. And that turned out to be a terrible mistake.

Outside, the wind was picking up ground speed and scattering fence posts as it went.

"Willjillhesterchesterpeterpollytimtommarylarryandlittleclarinda!" I shouted. "Inside, my lambs. That wind is getting ornery!"

The young 'uns came trooping in and pulled off their windshoes. And not a moment too soon. The clothes-line began to whip around so fast it seemed to disappear. Then we saw a hen-house come flying through the air, with the hens still in it.

The sky was turning dark and mean. The wind came out of the far north, howling and shrieking and shaking the house. In the cupboard, cups chattered in their saucers.

Soon we noticed big balls of fur rolling along the prairie like tumbleweeds. Turned out they were timber wolves from up north. And then an old hollow log came spinning across the farm and split against my chopping-stump. Out rolled a black bear, and was he in a temper! He had been trying to hibernate and didn't take kindly to being awakened. He gave out a roar and looked around for somebody to chase. He saw us at the windows and decided we would do.

The mere sight of him scared the young 'uns and they huddled together, holding hands, near the fireplace.

I got down my shotgun and opened a window. That was a *mistake!* Two things happened at once. The bear was coming on and in my haste I forgot to calculate the direction of the wind. It came shrieking along the side of the house and when I poked the gun-barrel out of the window, well, the wind bent it like an angle iron. That buck-shot flew due south. I found out later it brought down a brace of ducks over Mexico.

But worse than that, when I threw open the window such a draught came in that our young 'uns *were sucked up through the chimney!* Holding hands, they were carried away like a string of sausages.

Mama near fainted away. "My dear Melissa," I exclaimed. "Don't you worry! I'll get our young 'uns back!"

I fetched a rope and rushed outside. I could see the young 'uns up in the sky and blowing south.

I could also see the bear and he could see me. He gave a growl with a mouthful of teeth like rusty nails. He rose up on his hind-legs and came towards me with his eyes glowing red as fire.

I didn't fancy tangling with that monster. I dodged around

31

behind the clothes-line. I kept one eye on the bear and the other on the young 'uns. They were now flying away over the county and hardly looked bigger than Mayflies.

The bear charged towards me. The wind was spinning the clothes-line so fast he couldn't see it. And he charged smack into it. My, didn't he begin to jump! He jumped red-hot pepper, only faster. He had got himself trapped inside the rope and couldn't jump out.

Of course, I didn't lose a moment. I began flapping my arms like a bird. That was such an enormous *big* wind I figured I could fly after the young 'uns. The wind tugged and pulled at me, but it couldn't lift me an inch off the ground.

Tarnation! I had eaten too many biscuits. They were heavy as lead and weighed me down.

The young 'uns were almost out of sight. I rushed to the barn for the wind-plough. Once out in the breeze, the bed-sheet filled with wind. Off I shot like a cannon-ball, ploughing a deep furrow as I went.

Didn't I streak along, though! I was making better time than the young 'uns. I kept my hands on the plough handles and steered around barns and farmhouses. I saw hay-stacks explode in the wind. If that wind got any stronger it wouldn't surprise me to see the sun blown off course. It would set in the south at high noon.

I ploughed right along and gained rapidly on the young 'uns. They were still holding hands and just clearing the tree-tops. Before long I was within hailing distance.

"Be brave, my lambs," I shouted. "Hold tight!"

I spurted after them until their shadows lay across my path. But the bed-sheet was so swelled out with wind that I couldn't

stop the plough. Before I could let go of the handles and jump off I had sailed far *ahead* of the young 'uns.

I heaved the rope into the air. "Willjillhesterchesterpeterpollytimtommarylarryandlittleclarinda!" I shouted as they came flying overhead. "Hang on!"

34

Hester missed the rope, and Jill missed the rope, and so did Peter. But Will caught it. I had to dig my heels in the earth to hold them. And then I started back. The young 'uns were too light for the wind. They hung in the air. I had to drag them home on the rope like balloons on a string.

Of course it took most of the day to shoulder my way back through the wind. It was a mighty struggle, I tell you! It was near supper-time when we saw our farmhouse ahead, and that black bear was still jumping rope!

I dragged the young 'uns into the house. The rascals! They had had a jolly time flying through the air, and wanted to do it again! Mama put them to bed with their wind-shoes on.

The wind blew all night, and the next morning that bear was still jumping rope. His tongue was hanging out and he had lost so much weight he was skin and bones.

Finally, about mid-morning, the wind got tired of blowing one way, so it blew the other. We got to feeling sorry for that bear and cut him loose. He was so tuckered out he didn't even growl. He just pointed himself towards the tall timber to find another hollow log to crawl into. But he had lost the fine art of walking. We watched him jump, jump, jump north until he was out of sight.

That was the howlin', scowlin', all mighty *big* wind that broke my leg. It had not only pulled up fence posts, but the *holes* as well. It dropped one of those holes right outside the barn door and I stepped in it.

That's the bottom truth. Everyone on the prairie knows Josh McBroom would rather break his leg than tell a fib.

MᶜBROOM's
EAR

Grasshoppers – yes, they did get wind of our wonderful one-acre farm. The long-legged, saw-legged, hop-legged rascals ate us out of house and home.

You know how grasshoppers are. They'd as soon spit tobacco juice as look at you. And they're terrible hungry creatures. I guess there's nothing that can eat more in less time than a swarm of grasshoppers. Green things, especially, make their mouths water.

I don't intend to talk about it with a hee and a haw. Mercy, no! If you know me – Josh McBroom – you know I'd as soon live in a tree as tamper with the truth.

I'd best start with the weather. Summer was just waking up, but the days weren't near warm enough yet for grass-hoppers. The young 'uns were helping me to dig a water-well. They talked of growing one thing and another to enter in the County Fair.

I guess you've heard how amazing rich our farm was. Any-thing would grow in it – quick. Seeds would burst in the ground and crops would shoot right up before your eyes. Why, just yesterday our oldest boy dropped a five-cent piece and before he could find it that nickel had grown to a quarter.

Early one morning a skinny, tangle-haired stranger came ambling along the road. My, he was tall! I do believe if his hat fell off it would take a day or two to reach the ground.

"Howdy, sir," he said. "I'm Slim-Face John from here, there, and other places. I'll paint your barn cheap."

That man was not only tall, skinny, and tangle-haired, he was near-sighted. "We don't own a barn," I said.

He squinted and laughed. "In that case," he said, "I'll paint it free."

"Done," I smiled.

He painted that no-barn in less than a second, with time left over. He appeared to be hungry, so my dear wife, Melissa, gave him a hearty breakfast and he went ambling away. "I'll be back." He waved.

The young 'uns and I kept digging that well. My, it was hard work. They'd lower a bucket, I'd fill it with earth, and they'd haul it up like a tug-of-war. All eleven of them.

The days grew longer and hotter. Flies began to drop out of the air with sun-stroke.

But it still wasn't grasshopper weather.

"Will*jill*hester*chester*peter*polly*tim*tom*marylarryandlittle-*clarinda!*" I had to shout from the bottom of the well. "Work to do! Haul up the bucket!"

"Aw, Pa," Chester complained from the tree-house. "I'm fixin' to grow a prize water-melon for the Fair. A fifty-pounder."

"I think I'll grow a pumpkin," Polly said.

"Well, I'm growing impatient!" I said. "Haul up the bucket, my lambs, and dump it. County Fair's still a week off."

The next day was a real sizzler. At high noon the yellow wax beans began melting on the vines. They dripped like candles.

No – it wasn't grasshopper weather yet. The leggy creatures
would catch cold on a chilly day like that.

We finished the well at last, with the bucketfuls of earth
standing in a big heap beside it. Along about supper-time
that tall, skinny, tangle-haired, near-sighted stranger was
back.

"Howdy," he said. "I'm Slim-Face John from here, there,
and other places. I'll dig you a water-well cheap."

"We've got a well," I said.

"In that case," he answered, "I'll dig it free."

He stayed for supper and then went ambling away. "I'll be
back." He waved.

Another day passed. The sun-ball began to outdo itself.
Hot? Why, the next morning it was so infernal hot that a
block of ice felt warm to the touch. Mama had to boil water
to cool it off. Sunflowers along the road picked up their roots
and hurried under the trees for shade.

That was grasshopper weather.

Just after breakfast the first jumpers arrived. They came

39

in twos and fours. Our farm stood green as an emerald and it was bound to catch their eye. Before long they were turning up in sixes and eights.

I must admit those first visitors surprised us with their nice table manners. They didn't spit tobacco juice any which way. Peter set out an old coffee can and they used it for a spittoon.

By noon hop-legs were arriving by the fifties and hundreds. They nibbled our cabbage and lettuce, but it was nothing to be alarmed about. We could grow vegetables faster than they could eat them – three or four crops a day.

Along about sundown the saw-legged visitors came whirring in by the hundreds and the thousands. I wasn't worried. Grasshoppers are hardly worth counting in small numbers like that.

"Pa," Chester said at breakfast. "County Fair's tomorrow. Reckon it's time to set out my water-melons."

"I'm going to grow a prize tomato," Mary declared. "Big as a balloon."

"You young 'uns use the patch behind the house," I said. "I aim to plant the farm in corn."

The grasshoppers didn't get in our way. Larry and little Clarinda fed them turnip greens out of their hands. I got the field planted in no time.

My, it was fine corn-growing weather. The stalks leapt right up, dangling with ears.

Suddenly a silvery green cloud rose off the horizon and raced towards us.

Grasshoppers!

Grasshoppers by the thousands! Grasshoppers by the millions! Little did we know it was the beginning of the Great

Grasshopper War – or, as it came to be called, the War of McBroom's Ear.

"Will*jill*hester*chester*peter*polly*tim*tom*mary*larry*andlittle-*clarinda*!" I shouted. "Brooms and branches! Shoo them off!"

We began yelling and running about and waving our weapons. The grasshoppers spun over our ripening cornfield. They feasted their eyes – and flew off.

"We – scared 'em away!" Tim declared.

"No," I said. "That was just the advance party. They went back for the main herd. *And here they come!*"

Acres of grasshoppers! Square miles of grasshoppers! They came streaking towards us like a great roaring thunderbolt of war.

"Brooms and branches!" I yelled.

The hungry devils tucked napkins under their chins and swooped down for the attack. Mercy! The air got so thick with hoppers you could swing a bucket once and fill it twice. They made a whirring, hopping, jumping fog. We could barely see a foot beyond our noses.

But we could hear the ravenous rascals. They were chomping and chewing up our cornfield and spitting out the cobs. They ate that farm right down to the ground in exactly four seconds flat.

Then they rose in the air, still hungry as wolves, and waited for the next crop.

"Pa!" Chester said. "They skinned my water-melons!"

"Pa!" Mary cried. "They didn't even wait for my tomatoes to ripen. They ate them green!"

"Pa!" little Clarinda said. "What happened to your socks?"

I looked down. Glory be! Those infernal dinner guests had eaten the socks right out of my shoes – green socks. All they left were the holes in the toes.

Some of the young 'uns broke into tears. "We won't be able to grow anything for the County Fair!"

"We're not beat yet, my lambs," I said, thinking as hard as I could. "Those hoppers did have us outnumbered, but not outsmarted. I'm going to town for seed. Better clear away the corn-cobs."

I drove to town in our air-cooled Franklin automobile and was back before noon with fifty pounds of fine seed. The grasshoppers were still stretched all over the sky, waiting. The young 'uns had cleared the farm, throwing the corn-cobs on the heap of dirt beside the well.

"Not a moment to lose," I said. "Help scatter the seed."

Before long our farm was bushed out, green as a one-acre jungle. Those hoppers smacked their lips and fought to get at it. They whirred and swarmed and cranched and crunched – that crop disappeared as if sucked up by a tornado.

Well, you should have seen how surprised they were! That first wave of hoppers was all but breathing fire. And no wonder. They had dined on hot green peppers.

They streaked off in a hurry, looking for something to drink.

Of course, there were still tons of grasshoppers left. We kept sowing crops of hot green peppers all afternoon until there wasn't a jump-leg to be seen. We found out later they had swarmed to a lake in the next county and drunk it dry.

But they'd be back. The young 'uns would have to grow their prizewinners in a hurry.

"Pa – look!" little Clarinda shouted.

She was pointing to the tall heap of dirt, littered with corn-cobs. Glory be! The grasshoppers had missed a lone kernel and it had taken root behind our backs. A cornstalk was growing up as big as a tree.

That dirt hill was powerful rich. The roots of that wondrous stalk were having a banquet! A single ear of corn began to form before our eyes. Big? Why, it was already fatter than a pot-bellied stove and still growing.

"That looks like a prizewinner to me!" I declared. "You scamps will go partners."

Jill and Hester and Polly climbed to their tree-house to keep a sharp eye out for grasshoppers. That ear of corn grew longer and fatter. It was a beauty! The stalk began to bend under its weight. And it was ripening fast.

Didn't we get busy, though! We fixed loops of rope around that ear so as to let it down easy. Will climbed up a ladder with a bucksaw and went to work. It must have taken him five minutes to saw that giant ear off the stalk.

We eased it down with the ropes. I tell you, we could hardly believe our eyes. That ear of corn was so big you couldn't see it in a single glance. You had to look twice.

"Grasshoppers!" Jill shouted from the tree-house. "Grasshoppers coming, Pa!"

"Quick," I said. "Into the house!"

It took all of us to lift that ear of corn. But it wouldn't

fit through the door. And it wouldn't fit through the window.

"The well!" I shouted.

We lowered it by ropes and covered the well over with some rusty sheets of corrugated tin. And just in time. Those hoppers had spotted our great ear from the sky and came whirring across the farm in a green blizzard. But they couldn't get at that ear of corn.

"It's safe for the night," I said.

"How will we *ever* get it past the hoppers to the Fair to-morrow?" Mary asked.

I don't have to tell you the problem gave me a sleepless night. About four in the morning I jumped out of bed and woke the young 'uns.

"Brooms and buckets!" I said. "Follow me."

We tiptoed outside, careful not to wake the jump-legs. We quietly raised our ear of corn from the well and replaced the sheets of corrugated tin. Then I filled the buckets from the shed.

"Start painting," I whispered.

The young 'uns dipped their brooms and painted that giant ear from end to end and all over.

At sun-up the grasshoppers rose from the fields and went looking for breakfast. They headed straight for the well, banging their heads on the rusty tin. My, what a clatter! They thought our enormous big ear was still down there.

Well, it was in plain sight. Only they didn't recognize it. The husk wasn't green any more. We had *whitewashed* it.

We lifted it to the roof of the old Franklin and tied it down. "Everybody pile in." I smiled, starting up the motor. "We're off to the Fair!"

45

Just then Mr. Slim-Face John came along.

"Howdy." He smiled. "I'll paint your farmhouse cheap."

"Oh, I'd dearly like that," Mama said. "Red, with white window-sills."

"Done," I said. "You'll find paint in the shed." And we were off.

Well, you should have seen heads turn along the way. What *was* that thing on the roof of our car? An ear of corn? No sir! No farmer can raise corn that big. And white as chalk!

We bumped along the dirt road, following signs to the County Fair. We enjoyed the sights – barns, and silos, and cows chewing their cuds in the shade.

"How much farther?" Polly asked.

"Ten, twelve miles," I said. "Be patient."

I noticed the prairie windmills begin to turn. A hot wind was coming up, dragging a cloud with it. We could hear the rumble of thunder.

"How much farther, Pa?" Tim asked.

"Eight, ten miles," I said. "Be patient."

But I didn't like the look of that cloud. It grew darker and heavier and came blowing our way

"Heads in!" I called to the young 'uns. "Thunder shower ahead."

We met the storm head on. It didn't amount to much, but those raindrops were almost hot enough to scald you. They bounced like sparks off the hood. A moment later the sky was blue again and the summer shower behind us.

"How much farther, Pa?" Mary asked.

"Six, eight miles," I said. "Be patient."

"Pa," Will said. He hadn't bothered to pull his head in out

46

of the window and his hair was wet. "Pa, look what's happened to our corn!"

I jammed on the brakes and got out to see. Lo and behold – the husk was bright green again! The summer shower had washed off the whitewash.

I jumped back behind the wheel and off we spun. "Watch for grasshoppers," I shouted.

"I'm watching, Pa," little Clarinda answered. "*And here they come!*"

Well, it was a race. The hoppers came roaring after us in full battle formation. The old Franklin creaked and groaned and clanked, but her heart was in it. We bumped in and out of the ruts and jumped a few.

"They're gaining on us, Pa!"

I had the foot pedal to the floorboard. Soon we could see the flags and banners of the County Fair ahead.

But not soon enough. The first hop-legs were landing on the roof and we could hear them ripping and tearing at the husk. By the time we reached the fairgrounds we'd have nothing left but the cob.

But the old Franklin started to back-fire, banging and booming something fierce. Those hop-legs jumped a mile and we made it across the fairgrounds.

I charged right into the main-exhibition building and jammed on the brakes. "Shut all the doors!" I shouted. "Grasshoppers! Grasshoppers coming!"

The doors swung shut and we could breathe easy at last. Folks began to cluster around, their eyes rising as their jaws fell open at the wonder of our ear of corn. And I declare if the hungry rascals hadn't husked it neat as you please.

We lifted it down off the roof and put it on display on two picnic tables. The judges came by and asked what name to enter it by.

"McBroom." I smiled. "Will*jill*hester*chester*peter*polly*tim-*tom*mary*larry*andlittle*clarinda* – McBroom!"

Well, the judges gave it first, second, third prize and honourable mention, too. But, my, it was getting overheated in there with the doors closed.

The young 'uns lined up to have their picture taken for the county paper. There was one long smile reaching from Will at one end to little Clarinda at the other. The noon sun kept beating down on the roof and of a sudden there came a loud bang.

I thought at first it was our tired old Franklin. But no.

48

It was the young 'uns' enormous, big prize-winning ear of corn – beginning to pop! The inside of that building had grown so infernal hot it was a perfect popcorn popper.

Well, it did get noisy in there! Kernels swelled and exploded like great white cannon-balls. They bounced off the roof and the walls. Pop-pop-pop. Pop. Pop-pop-pop-pop-pop! Folks ducked and others ran. Corn in their rows boomed away in regular broadsides! I tell you popcorn was flying all over the hall and piling up like a heavy snowfall. Pop-pop-pop-pop-pop-pop-pop-pop! In no time at all we were buried in light, fluffy popcorn. It swelled to the roof and forced open the doors. It overflowed the building at both ends.

There wasn't a grasshopper left in sight. All that ruckus had sent them flying. As far as I know they headed for the full moon. Must have heard it was made of green cheese. We never saw them again.

We stayed the afternoon – everyone did. Folks melted up buckets of prize butter and someone went to town for barrels of salt. There was more than enough fresh popcorn to go round. Salted and buttered, it was delicious. One piece was enough to feed an entire family.

Did I tell you I'd as soon live in a tree as tamper with the truth? Well, when we got back that night we found our farmhouse chawed and gnawed and eaten to the ground. Mr. Slim-Face John was not only tall, skinny, tangle-haired, and near-sighted. He was also colour-blind. Painted our house green.

Yes – it's a mite crowded living up here in the young 'uns' tree-house. But those prize ribbons – they're all mighty nice to look at.

McBROOM'S GHOST

Ghosts? Mercy, yes – I can tell you a thing or three about ghosts. As sure as my name's Josh McBroom a haunt came lurking about our wonderful one-acre farm.

I don't know when that confounded dry-bones first moved in with us, but I suspicion it was when we built our new home. Then winter set in. An *uncommon* cold winter it was,

50

too, though not so cold that an honest man would tell fibs about it. Still, you had to be careful when you lit a match. The flame would freeze and you had to wait for a thaw to blow it out.

Some old-timers declared that was just a middling cold winter out here on the prairie. Nothing for the record books. Still, we did lose our rooster, Sillibub. He jumped on the woodpile, opened his beak to crow the break of day and the poor thing quick-froze as stiff as glass.

The way I reckoned it, that ghost was whisking about and got ice-bound on our farm.

The young 'uns were the first to discover the pesky creature. A March thaw had come along and they had gone outside to play. I was bundled up in bed with the laryngitis – hadn't been able to speak above a whisper for three days. I passed the time listening to John Philip Sousa's band on our talking-machine. My, those piccolos did sound pretty!

Suddenly, the young 'uns were back and they appeared kind of strange in the eyes.

"Pa," said our youngest boy, Larry. "Pa, do roosters ever turn into ghosts?"

I tried to clear my throat. "Never heard of such a thing," I croaked.

"But we just this minute heard old Sillibub *crow*," said our oldest girl, Jill.

"Impossible, my lambs," I whispered, and they went out to frolic in the sun again.

I cranked up the talking-machine and once more Mr. Sousa's band came marching and trilling out of the morning-glory horn. Suddenly the young 'uns were back – all eleven of them.

51

"We heard it again," said Will.

"*Cock-a-doodle-do!*" little Clarinda crowed. "Plain as day, Pa. Out by the woodpile."

I shook my head. "Must be Mr. Sousa's piccolos you're hearing," I said hoarsely, and they went out to play again.

I cranked up the machine and before I knew it the young 'uns came flocking back in.

"Yes, Pa?" Will said.

"Yes, Pa?" Jill said.

"You called, Pa?" Hester said.

I lifted the needle off the record and gazed at them. "Called?" I croaked. Then I laughed hoarsely. "Why, you scamps know I can't raise my voice above a whisper. Aren't you full of mischief today!"

"But we *heard* you, Pa," Chester said.

"'Will*jill*hester*chester*peter*polly*tim*tom*mary*larry*andlittle-*clarinda!*'" Polly said. "It was your very own voice, Pa. And plain as day."

Well, after that they wouldn't go back out to play. They were certain some scaresome thing was roving about. Sure enough, the next morning we were awakened at dawn by the crowing of a rooster. It *did* sound like old Sillibub. But I said, "Heck Jones must have got himself a rooster. That's what we hear."

"But Heck Jones doesn't keep chickens," my dear wife Melissa reminded me. "You know he's raising hogs, Pa. The meanest, wildest hogs I ever saw. I do believe he hopes they'll root up our farm and drive us out."

Heck Jones was our neighbour, and an almighty torment to us. He was tall and scrawny and just as mean and ornery as

those Arkansas razorback hogs of his. He'd tried more than once to get our rich one-acre farm for himself.

It wouldn't surprise me if he was making those queer noises himself. Well, if he thought he could scare us off our property he was mistaken!

By the time I got over the laryngitis the young 'uns were afraid to leave the house. They just stared out the windows. Something was out there. They were certain of it.

So I bundled up and marched outside to look for Heck Jones' footprints in the mud. Well, I had hardly got as far as the woodpile when a voice came ripping out of the still air.

"Will*jill*hester*chester*peter*polly*tim*tom*mary*larry*andlittle-
clarinda!"

That voice sounded *exactly* like my own. I spun about.

But there wasn't a soul to be seen.

I don't mind admitting that my hair shot up on end. It
knocked my hat off.

There wasn't a footprint to be seen, either.

"Do you think the farm is haunted?" Larry asked.

"No," I answered firmly. "Haunts clank chains and moan
like the wind and rap at doors."

Just then there came a rap at the door. The young 'uns all
shot looks at me – Mama too.

Well, I got up and opened the door and there was no one
there. That's when I had to admit there was a dry-bones

dodging about our property. And mercy, what a sly, prankster creature it was! When that ghost wasn't mimicking old Sillibub it was mimicking me.

Well, we didn't sleep very well after that. Some nights I didn't sleep at all. I kept a sharp eye out for that haunt, but it never would show itself.

Finally, Mama and the young 'uns began to talk about giving up the farm. Then we had another freeze and for three solid weeks that spirit didn't make a sound. We reckoned it had moved away.

We breathed easier, I can tell you! There was no more talk of leaving the farm. The young 'uns passed the time leafing through the mail order catalogue and we all listened to the talking-machine.

"Pa, we'd dearly love to have a dog," Jill said one day.

"You won't find dogs in the mail order catalogue, my lambs," I said.

"We know, Pa," said Chester. "But can't we have a dog? A big, shaggy farm dog?"

I shook my head sadly. A dog would be the ruination of our amazing rich one-acre farm. There was nothing that wouldn't grow in that remarkable soil of ours – and quicker'n scat. I thought back to the summer day little Clarinda had lost a baby tooth. By the time we found it that tooth had grown so large we had to put up a block and tackle to extract it.

"No," I said. "Dogs dig holes and bury bones. Those bones would grow the size of buried logs. I'm sorry, my lambs."

The icicles began to melt in the spring thaw – and there came another knock at the door.

55

The haunt was back!

That night the young 'uns slept huddled together all in one bed. Didn't I pace the floor, though! That door-rapping, rooster-crowing, me-mimicking dry-bones would drive us off our farm. Unless I drove it off first.

Early the next morning I trudged through the mud to town. Everyone said that the Widow Witherbee was a ghost seer.

I called on her first thing. She was a spry little cricket of a lady who bought and sold hand-me-down clothes. But tarnation! Her eyesight was failing and she said she couldn't spy out ghosts any more.

"What am I to do?" I asked, as a litter of mongrel pups nipped at my ankles.

"Simple," the Widow Witherbee said. "Burn a pile of old shoes. Never fails to drive ghosts away."

Well, that sounded like twaddle to me, but I was desperate. She went poking through rags and old clothes and I bought all the worn-out, hand-me-down shoes she could find.

"You'll also need a dog," she said.

My eyebrows shot up. "A dog?"

"Certainly," she said. "Certainly. How are you going to know if you ran off that haunt without a dog? Hounds can see ghosts. Mongrels are best. When their ears stand up and they freeze and point like a bird dog – you know they're staring straight at a ghost. Then you have to burn more shoes."

So I bought one of her flop-eared pups and started back for the farm, carrying a bushel basket of old shoes. As I approached the house I could see the young 'uns' faces at the windows. Piccolos were trilling merrily in the air.

56

But dash it all! When I opened the door I saw that no one had a record on the talking-machine.

"Confound that haunt!" I exploded. "Now it's imitating John Philip Sousa's entire marching band!"

Of course, the young 'uns couldn't believe I had brought home a dog. It was the first time all winter long I saw smiles on their faces. Didn't they gather around him, though! They promised to keep close watch so that he wouldn't bury any bones.

I didn't lose much time burning that bushel of old shoes. Mercy, what an infernal strong smell! I could imagine that dry-bones holding its nose and rattling away, never to return.

Every day after that we walked the pup around the farm and never once did he raise his flop-ears and point.

"By ginger!" I exclaimed finally. "The old shoes did it. That haunt is gone!"

By that time the young 'uns had decided on a name for the pup. They called him Zip. He grew up to be the handiest farm dog I ever saw. That rich soil of ours was rarin' to go and we started our spring planting – raised a crop of tomatoes and two crops of carrots the first day. In no time at all the young 'uns taught Zip to dig a furrow. Straight as a beeline, too!

But our troubles weren't over with that ghost chased off. One burning hot morning we planted the farm in corn. The stalks came busting up through the ground, leafing out and dangling with ears. I tell you, Heck Jones' hogs acted as if we had rung the dinner bell. Mercy! They came roaring down on us in a snorting, squealing, thundering herd.

"Will*jill*hester*chester*peter*polly*tim*tom*mary*larry*andlittle-*clarinda!*" I shouted. "*And* Zip! Run for your lives!"

Those hungry, half-wild razorback hogs broke down the stalks and gorged themselves on sweet ears of corn. Then they rooted up the farm looking for left-over carrots.

Well, those razorbacks finally trotted home, with their stomachs scraping the ground, and I followed along behind.

"Heck Jones," I said. He was standing in a cloud of flies and eating a shoofly pie. It was mostly made of molasses and

brown sugar, which attracted the flies and kept a body busy shooing them off. "Heck Jones, it appears to me you've been starving your hogs."

"Bless my soul, they don't look starved to me," he chuckled, shooing flies off his shoofly pie. "See for yourself, neighbour."

"Heck Jones," I said stoutly. "If you aim to raise hogs I'd advise you to grow your own hog feed."

"No need for that, neighbour," he laughed. "There's plenty of feed about and razorbacks can fend for themselves. Of course, if you hanker to give up farming I might make an offer for that patch of ground you're working."

"Heck Jones," I said for the last time. I could hardly see him for the cloud of flies. "You're mistaken if you think you and your razorbacks can drive us off, sir. Either pen up those hogs or I'll have the law on you!"

"There's no law says I've got to pen my hogs," he said, finishing off the pie and a few flies in the bargain. "Anyway, neighbour, no pen would hold the rascals."

Well, I'll admit he was right about that. We fenced our farm, but those infernal hogs busted through it and scattered the pieces like a cyclone. We strung barbed-wire. It only stopped them long enough to scratch their backs. Barbed wire was a *comfort* to those razorbacks.

I tell you we battled those hogs all spring and summer. We planted a crop of prickly pear cactus, but not even that kept the herd out. They ate the pears and picked their teeth with the prickly spines.

All the while Heck Jones stood on the brow of the hill eating shoofly pie and going, "Hee-*haw!* Hee-*haw!*" His hogs grew fatter and fatter. I tell you we were lucky to save enough food for our own table.

Another growing season like that and we'd be ruined!

Then summer came to an end and we knew we were in for more than an uncommon cold winter. It was going to be a *dreadful* cold winter. There were signs.

I remember that the boys had gone fishing in late October and brought home a catfish. *That catfish had grown a coat of winter fur.*

That wasn't all. After the first fall of snow, the young 'uns built a snowman. The next morning it was gone. We found out later that snowman had gone *south* for the winter.

Well, it turned out to be the Winter of the Big Freeze. I don't intend to stray from the facts, but I distinctly remember one day Polly dropped her comb on the floor and when she picked it up the teeth were chattering.

As things turned out, that was just a middling cold day in the Winter of the Big Freeze. The temperature kept dropping and I must admit some downright *unusual* things began to happen.

For one thing smoke took to freezing in the chimney. I had to blast it out with a shotgun three times a day. And we couldn't sit down to a bowl of Mama's hot soup before a crust of ice formed on top. The girls used to set the table with a knife, a fork, a spoon – and an ice-pick.

Well, the temperature kept dropping, but we didn't complain. At least there was no ghost lurking about and Heck Jones' hogs stayed home and the young 'uns had the dog to play with. I kept cranking the talking-machine.

Then the *big* freeze set in. Red barns for miles around turned blue with the cold. There's many an eye-witness to that!

One day the temperature fell so low that sunlight froze on the ground.

Now, I disbelieved that myself. So I scooped up a chunk in a frying-pan and brought it inside. Sure enough, I was able to read to the young 'uns that night by the glow of that frozen chunk of winter sun.

Of course, we had our share of wolves about. Many a night, through the windows, we could see great packs of them trying their best to howl. I suspicioned laryngitis. Those wolves couldn't make a sound. It was pitiful.

Well, spring thaw came at last. I remember stepping out-side and the first thing I heard was a voice.

"Hee-*haw!*"

"What mischief are you up to now, Heck Jones?" I ans-wered back.

But as I looked about me I saw there wasn't another soul on the farm.

Then I knew. My hair rose, knocking my hat to the ground again. That door-rapping, rooster-crowing, me-mimicking, hee-*hawing* ghost was back!

"Zip!" I shouted, and we went tracking all over the farm. Voices popped up behind us and in front of us and around the woodpile.

But that dog of ours never once lifted his flop-ears.

"Confound it!" I grumbled to Mama and the young 'uns. "Zip can't see ghosts at all!"

The poor mongrel knew I was dreadful disappointed in him. He lit out through my legs and dug a straight furrow in the farm quick as I ever saw. When that didn't bring a smile to my face, he zipped over to the corn bin and took a cob in his mouth. He'd watched us plant many a time. He ran back up the furrow, shelling the corn with his teeth and planting the kernels with a poke of his nose.

"Maybe Zip can't see ghosts," Will said. "But he's a power-ful smart farm dog, Pa. Can't we still keep him?"

I didn't have a moment to answer. As the cornstalks shot up, Heck Jones appeared eating a shoofly pie on the rim of the hill. At the same instant his razorback hogs came thundering towards us – and that infernal haunt began trilling like a piccolo.

"Run for your lives!" I shouted.

We all ran but Zip. The corn was ripening fast and he meant to *harvest* it.

I started back out-of-doors to snatch him up, but suddenly that prankish ghost changed its tune. It began howling like a pack of hungry wolves.

You never heard such a howling! And didn't those hogs stop in their tracks! I tell you they near jumped out of their skins. That ghost kept yipping and howling from every quarter. Heck Jones didn't have a chance to *hee* and to *haw*. Those razorbacks turned on their heels. They trampled him in the mud and kept running – though one of them did come back for the shoofly pie. My, they did run! I heard later they didn't stop until they arrived back in Arkansas where they were mistaken for guinea pigs. They had run off that much weight.

"Yes, my lambs," I said to the young 'uns. "Reckon we'll keep ol' Zip. Look at him harvest that corn!"

Well, we'd got rid of Heck Jones' razorback hogs, but we still had that dry-bones cutting up. The young 'uns remembered to be scared and streaked behind closed doors.

I stood my ground, scratching my head. Sounds were breaking out everywhere in the air. As if howling and yipping like an entire pack of wolves wasn't enough, that haunt joined in with Mr. Sousa's entire marching band. I must admit it had those piccolos down perfect.

I kept scratching my head and suddenly I said to myself, "Why, there's no haunt around here. No wonder ol' Zip couldn't spy it out."

Glory be! It was clear to me now. There never *had* been a haunt lurking about! It was nothing but the weather playing pranks on us. No wonder we hadn't been able to hear wolves in the dead of winter. *The sounds had frozen.*

And now all those sounds were *thawing* out!

Well, it wasn't long before I coaxed the young 'uns outside again, and soon they were enjoying the rappings at the door and the yips of wolves and shotgun blasts three times a day from the chimney-top.

And didn't they laugh about Heck Jones' razorback hogs running from the howling and yipping of last winter's wolves!

Well, that's the truth about our prairie winters and McBroom's ghost – as sure as I'm a truthful man.

64